To the parents of young children everywhere.

www.mascotbooks.com

Goodnight Box

For more information, please contact:
Mascot Books
620 Herndon Parkway, Suite 320
Herndon, VA 20170
info@mascotbooks.com

Library of Congress Control Number: 2020902840

CPSIA Code: PRTWP0720A
ISBN-13: 978-1-64543-318-7

Printed in South Korea

Goodnight Box

Michael B. Horn and Tracy Kim Horn

Illustrated by Agus Prajogo

In the big, bright box,
there is a whiteboard and a pull-up bar,

Junkyard dogs jumping over arms.

And there were angry gorillas deadlifting kettlebells

And two wooden rings awaiting their kip swings.

And a tall box jump and a fist bump.

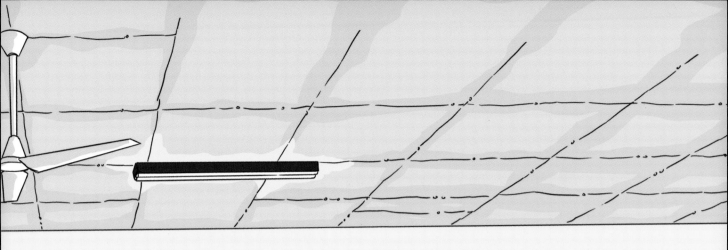

And a snatch and a sprint and one final lift.

And a fire-breathing coach who was oh-so-swift.

Goodnight box.

Goodnight arms.

Goodnight junkyard dogs jumping over arms.

Goodnight cleans and the pull-up bar.
Goodnight gorillas, goodnight kettlebells.

Goodnight rings,

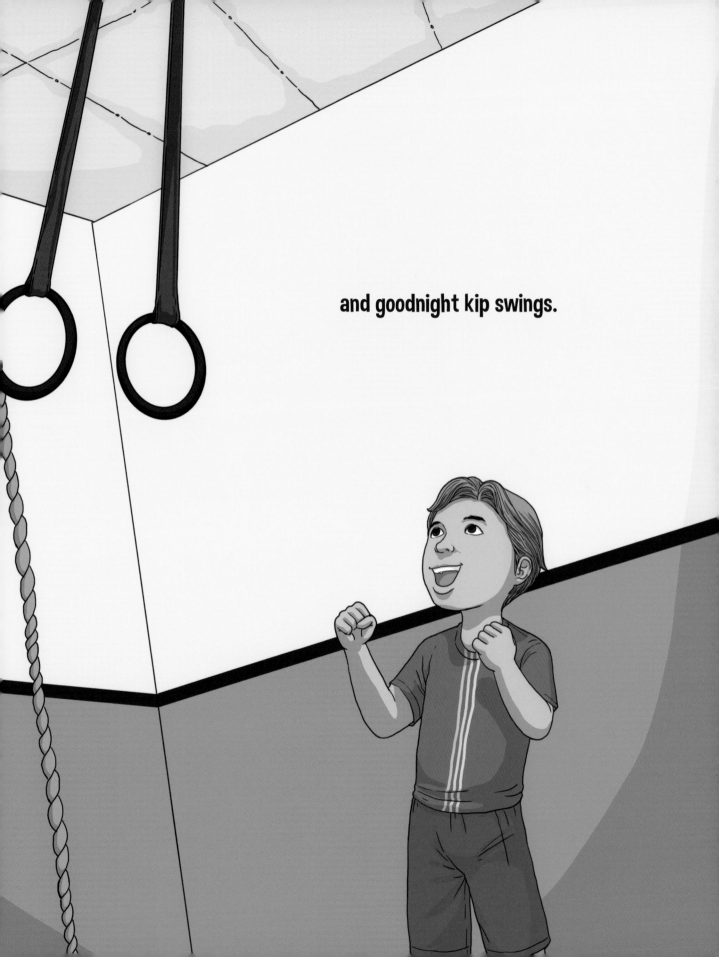

and goodnight kip swings.

Goodnight double under, and hello foam roller.

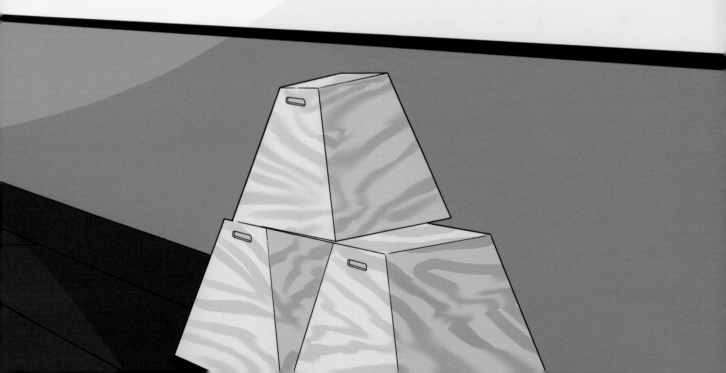

Goodnight tall box jump,

and goodnight fist bump.

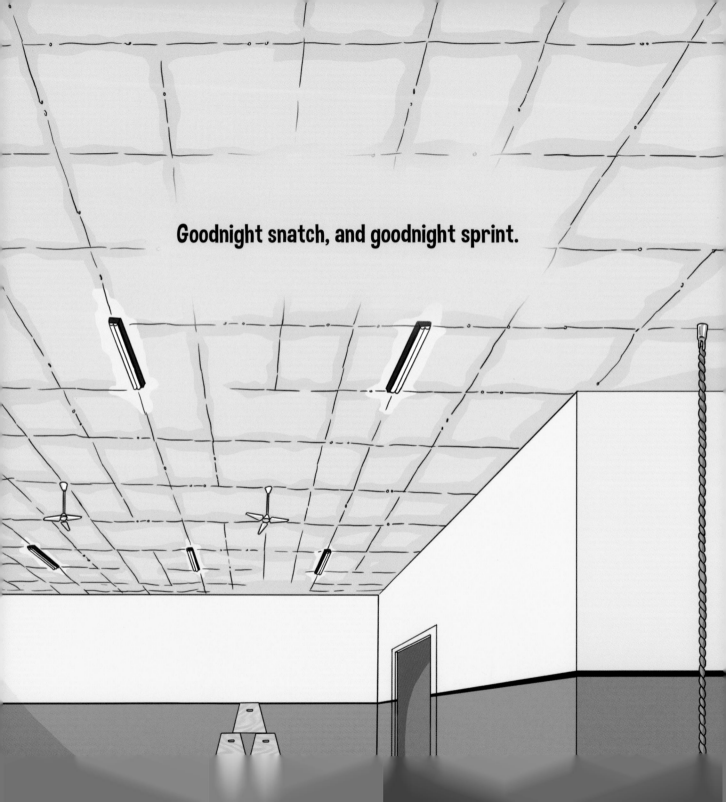

Goodnight snatch, and goodnight sprint.

Goodnight handstand walk.

Goodnight squats.

Goodnight athletes, see you mañana.